Do you still love me?

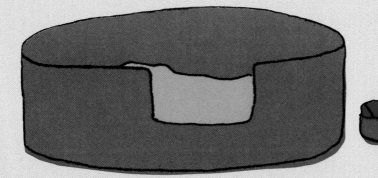

For Grandma

First U.S. edition 2003

First published in Great Britain by Gullane Children's Books

Library of Congress Cataloging-in-Publication Data is available.

Library of Congress Catalog Card Number 2003043835

ISBN 0-7636-2254-0

10 9 8 7 6 5 4 3 2 1

Printed in China

This book was typeset in Cafeteria-Bold.
The illustrations were done multimedia collage.

Candlewick Press
2067 Massachusetts Avenue
Cambridge, Massachusetts 02140

visit us at www.candlewick.com

Charlotte Middleton

Do you still love me?

CANDLEWICK PRESS
CAMBRIDGE, MASSACHUSETTS

Every morning, Dudley
liked to wake up early.

And every morning, he ate a hearty breakfast.

One of Dudley's favorite games was hide-and-seek.

He also liked to impress Aunt Prissy with his fleas.

WOOF!

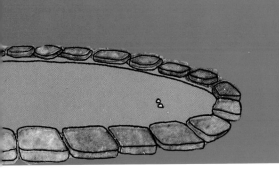

But most of all, Dudley liked
scaring Jenna, the neighbor's cat.

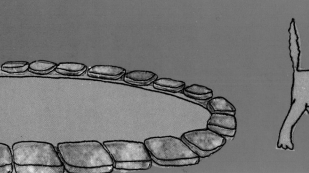

Every evening, Dudley and Anna curled up in their favorite place. It was the best part of the day.

Then one day, Anna brought home someone new—a baby chameleon called Pequito. From then on, things weren't the same.

Pequito got up even earlier than Dudley . . .

so Anna
did, too.

Pequito caught his
own breakfast . . .

and he was better
at hide-and-seek.

Pequito was even better at impressing Aunt Prissy,
although he didn't have fleas.

All of Anna's friends were fascinated by Pequito's big eyes.

And nobody noticed Dudley.

Worst of all, at the end of the day, there was now somebody else in Dudley's favorite place.

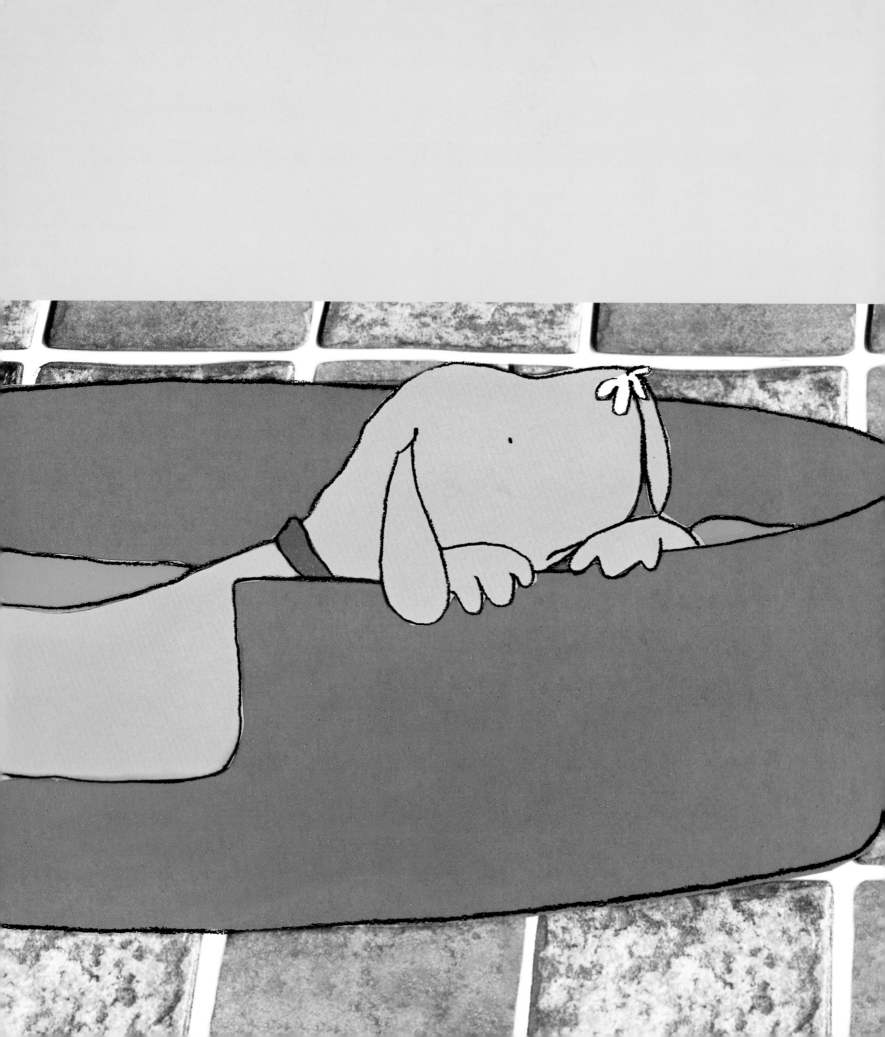

Dudley felt really sad.
Nobody seemed to care about him
anymore — only about Pequito
who was better at everything.

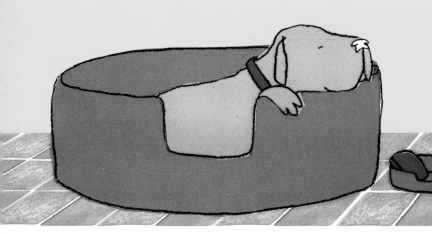

Later on, when Dudley woke up, Pequito was gone. Dudley was glad.

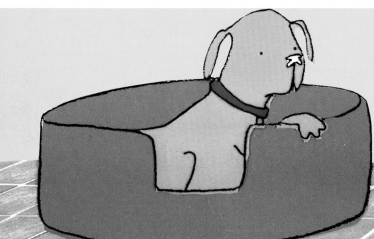

But when Pequito didn't come back, Dudley began to get worried.

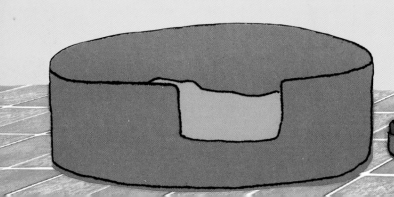

He decided to go looking.

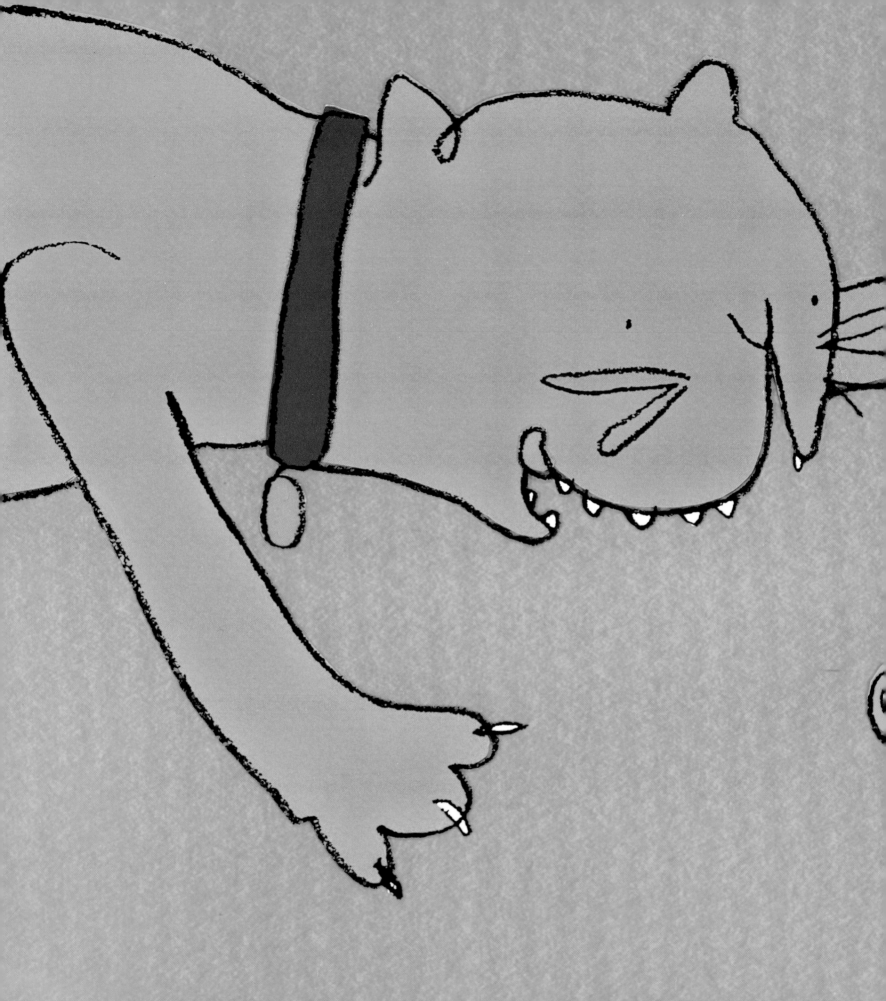

But somebody else had
already found Pequito.

Dudley barked louder than
he had ever barked before.

Anna and Pequito thought
Dudley was a hero!

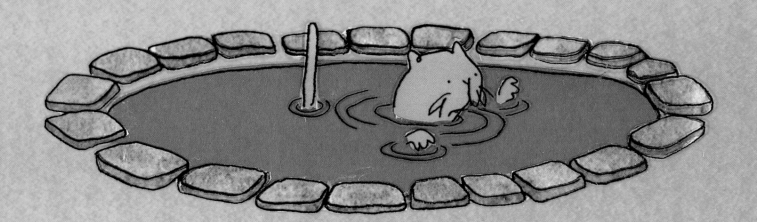

From then on, Dudley spent a lot of time doing something he was really good at . . .

looking after Pequito.